JUSTICE LEAGUE

THE SWARM

Writer: Brian Augustyn
Illustrator: Jason Armstrong Colorists: Dan Waters and Bill Friedenreich

Dalmatian Press, LLC, 2003. All rights reserved. Printed in the U.S.A.
The DALMATIAN PRESS name and logo are trademarks of Dalmatian Press, LLC, Franklin, Tennessee 37067.
No part of this book may be reproduced or copied in any form without the written permission from the copyright owner.

03 04 05 06 07 LBM 10 9 8 7 6 5 4 3 2
12546/JUSTICE LEAGUE: The Swarm

In the cold vacuum of space, Green Lantern was making mi
repairs to the Watchtower, Justice League's satellite headqua[r]
Suddenly, he saw an explosion on the moon!
He watched in horror as a cloud of dust—no! It was a horde
flying creatures!—burst through the moon's surface to fly stra[ight]
at him... and the Watchtower!

"Nothing lives on the moon," Green Lantern thought quickly. "...se must be visitors passing through—literally! It's as if ...ate right through the moon like giant termites! Is the ...chtower their next target?"

...he cloud of creatures swept blindly past the ...rald Guardian like a powerful river. ...reen lantern was so stunned that he ...t even have a chance to alert his ...w Justice Leaguers...

Inside the Watchtower, Superman and Wonder Woman greeted the Martian Manhunter who had just arrived safely in the teleportation tube. The green giant had been scouting a planet in a nearby galaxy, looking for signs of life.

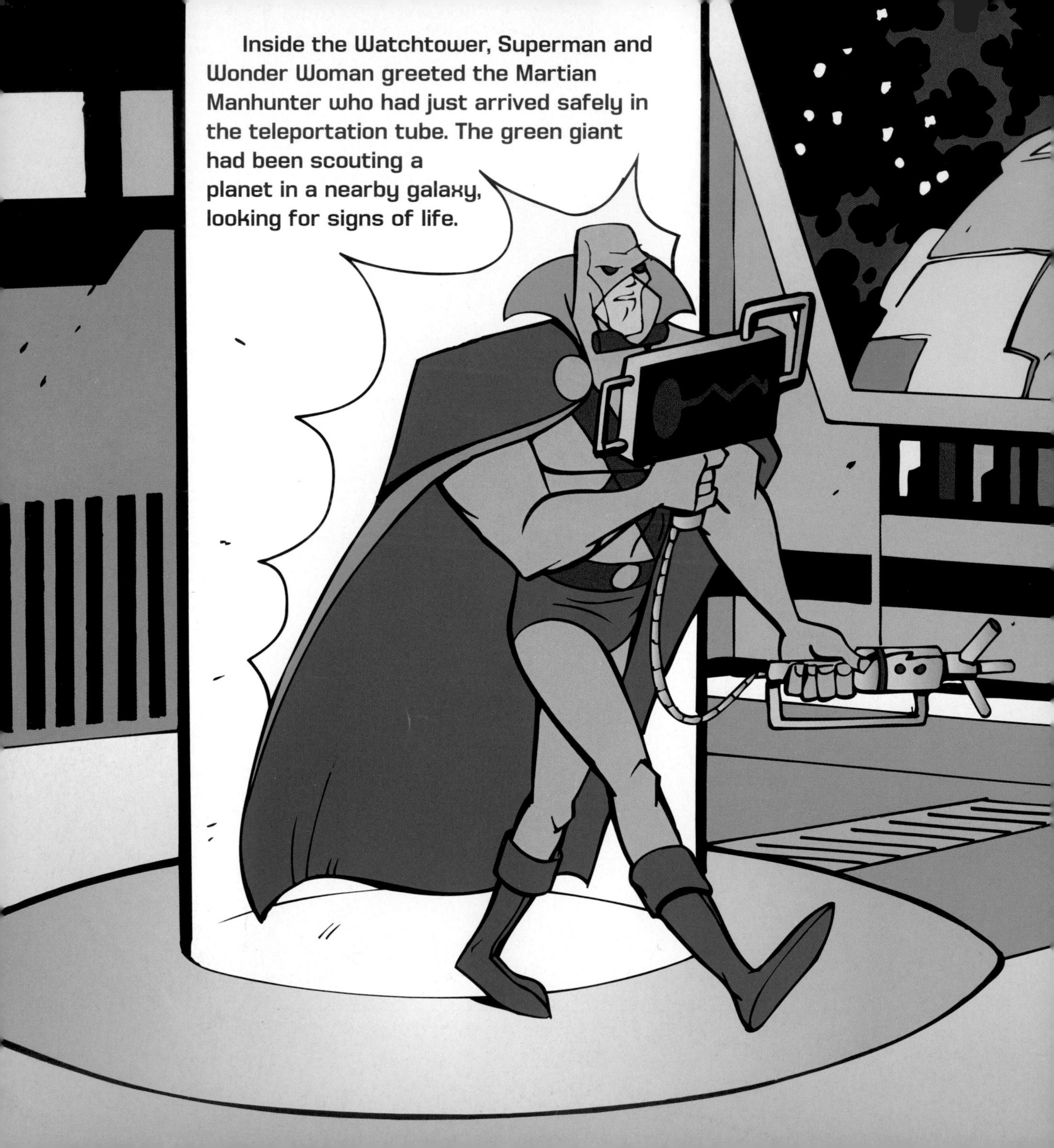

"Unfortunately," reported the Manhunter, "the newly discovered planet, T-4491, is completely without life forms. It is a world rich in metal ores, however, so we might one day be able to mine there."

"Well, that's up to S.T.A.R. Labs," Superman said with a smile. "We just agreed to scout the place."

"And it was a good chance to test our new teleportation chamber," said Wonder Woman.

Even Green Lantern's mighty emerald energy couldn't stop all t[he] speeding, swarming creatures!

"They're like army ants on the march!" marveled Green Lantern. "They're unstoppable!"

"Look out! We're being invaded by a swarm of alien bugs!" warned the surprised Flash.

"They've already eaten through a lot of our power system—including the teleporter circuits!" the Scarlet Speedster told his shocked teammates.

"These creatures are going to eat us out of house and home! We have to stop them!" shouted Wonder Woman. "Where are you going, Flash?"

"To fix the teleporter!" the speeding Flash called back.

"Don't worry about our safety now. We can't let them reach Earth!" said Superman.

"I saw what they did to the moon," said Green Lantern. "These bugs can destroy a world from the inside, like worms in an appl

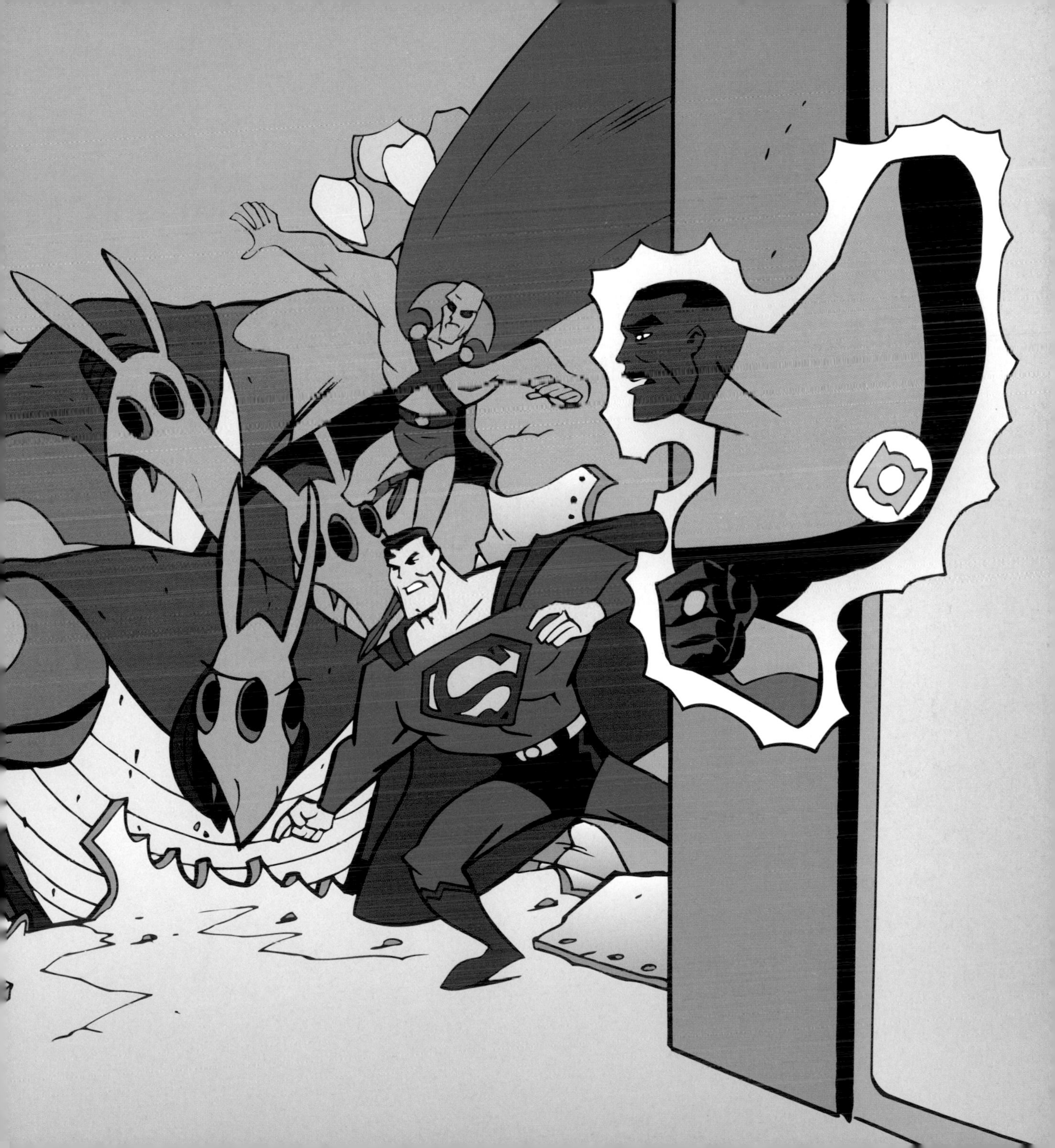

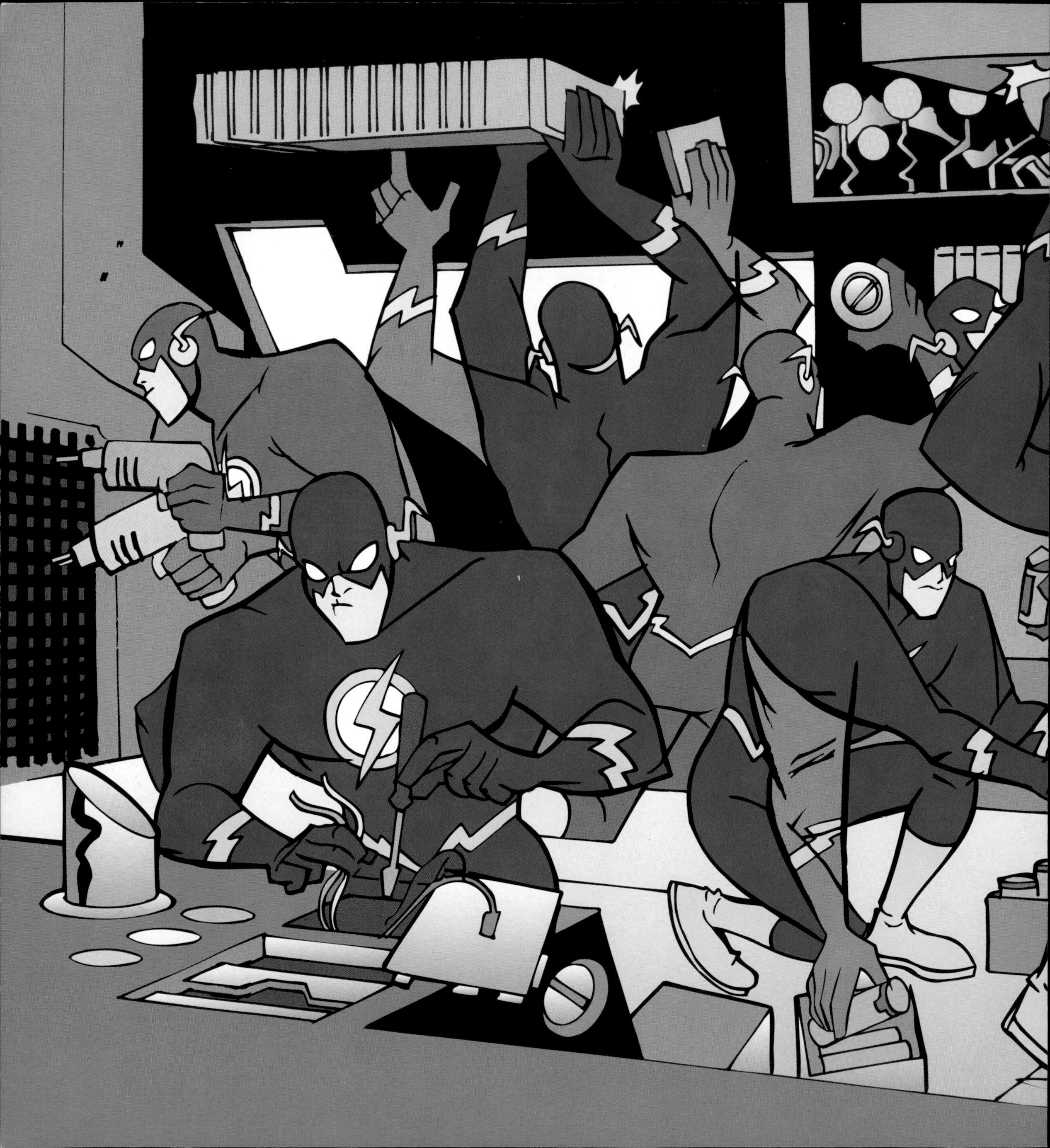

Inside a maze of repair passages, the Flash worked super swiftly to restore the Watchtower's power. He moved so fast he seemed to be everywhere at once!

"Doesn't Flash care that we're under attack?" wondered Green Lantern. "We need his help fighting these creatures!"

"It's not like him to be worrying about escape. He's not a coward... is he?" asked Wonder Woman.

In the League's meeting room, Superman and Martian Manhunter combined their extraordinary superbreaths to whip up a miniature hurricane. The creatures escaped by eating right through the walls!

"They're chewing through steel as if it were br gasped Wonder Woman.

"We have to find a way to put these pests on diet—and soon!" said Green Lantern.

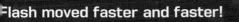

Flash moved faster and faster!

But would the fastest man alive be quick enough to save the day?

The alien creatures were as slippery as wet fish and as powerful as a herd of charging elephants. They rushed on, not caring what—or who—was in their way!

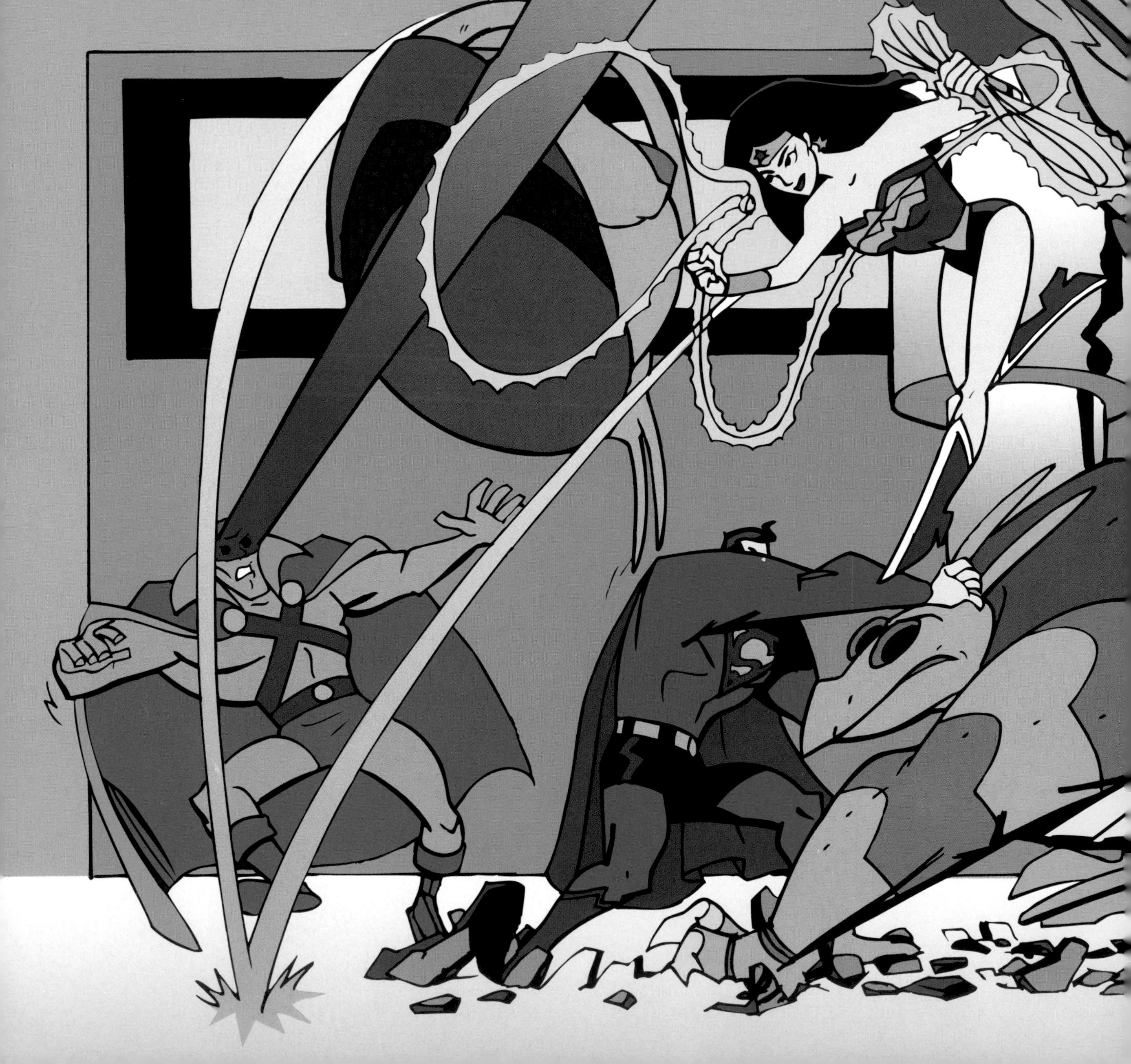

The mighty Justice League wondered if their great powers were enough to stop this alien swarm.

With his power ring, Green Lantern created mirror-images of the creatures, hoping to slow them down. But his trick backfired, and the creatures ate through the deck in a panic to escape their green duplicates.

"We have to hold them back," shouted Wonder Woman.
they get through, Earth will be their next meal!"
"They'll destroy the entire planet!" said Superman.
"It would be nice to have Flash's help," Green Lantern
d. "Where is he?"

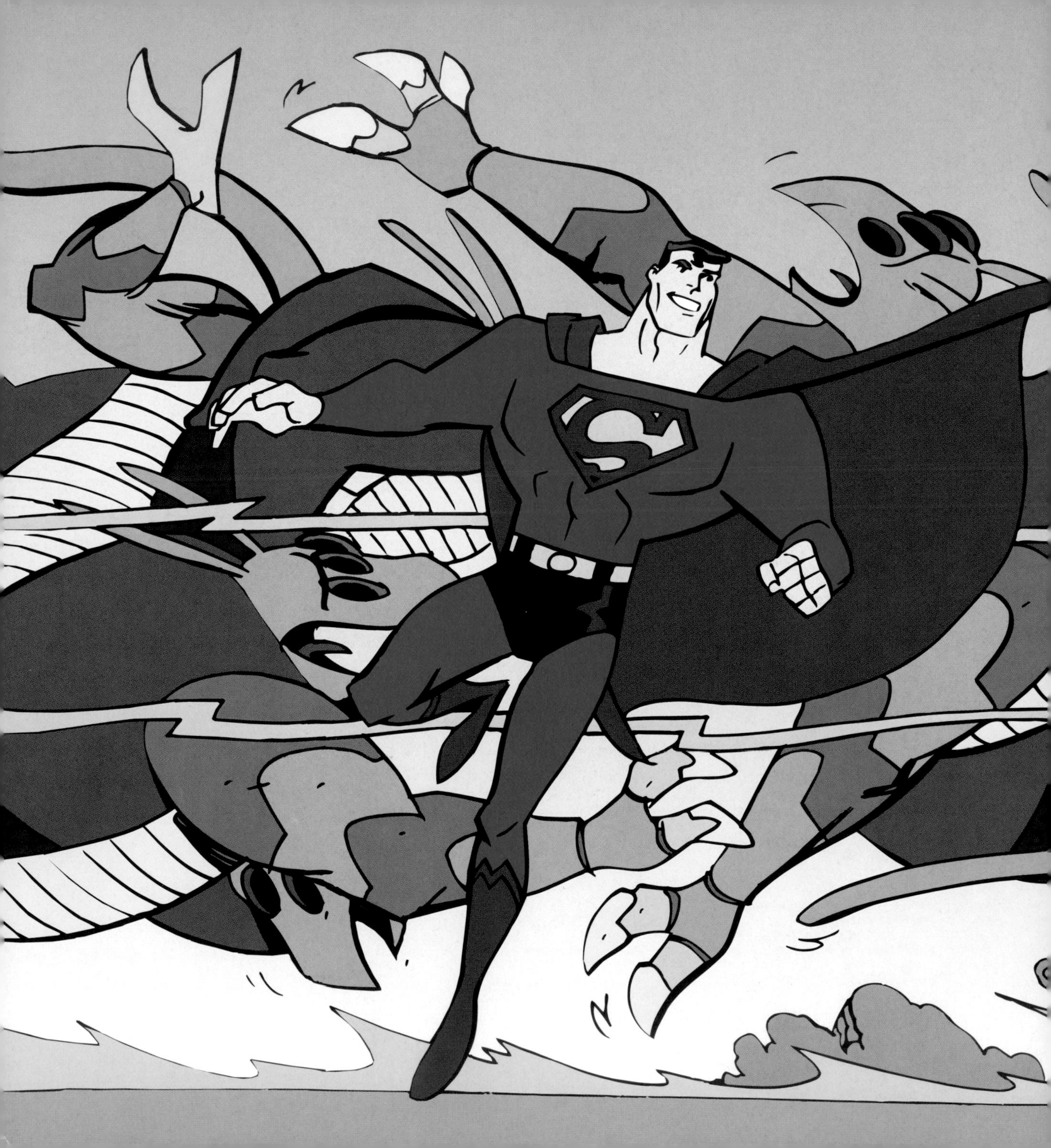

As though in answer, Flash sped into the room—only to zoom out again, dragging the creatures helplessly along!

What was the speedster planning?

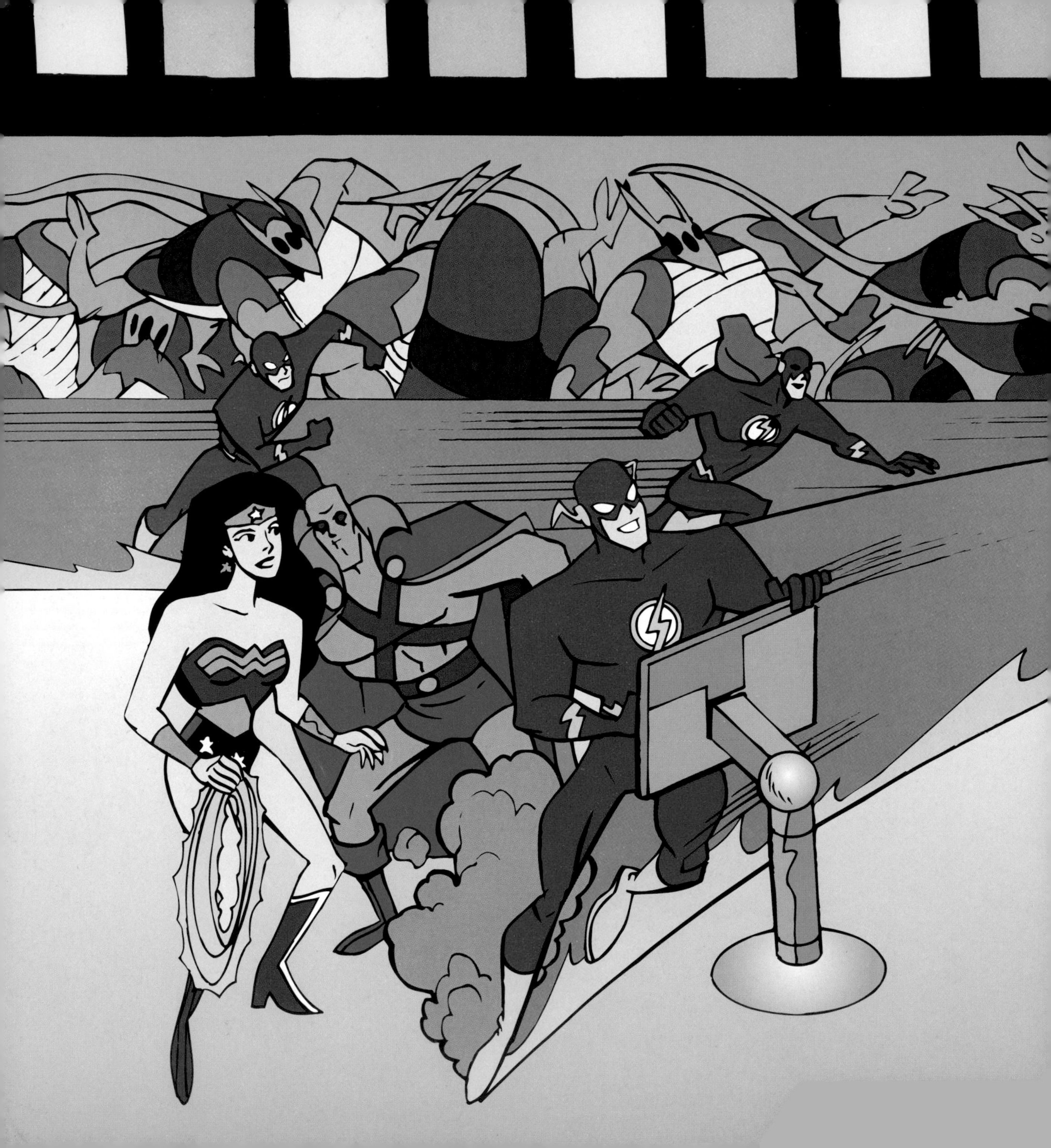

"I got the teleporter working again—just for them," said Flash with a happy grin. "Next stop: outta' here!"

"Where did you send them?" asked a concerned Martian Manhunter.

"To the uninhabited planet you explored this morning, J'onn!" answered Flash.

"The planet is eight times bigger than Earth," said the Manhunter. "Big enough to feed even these hungry creatures for hundreds of years."

"They seem to like it," said Wonder Woman with relief.

"And," said Superman, "we can keep an eye on them to make sure they never go wandering again."

"Quick thinking, Flash," said Wonder Woman.
"Speed is his specialty, after all," said Superma
"But even Flash isn't fast enough to get out of
cleaning up the mess those big bugs left behind,"
added Green Lantern, with a wink.